WHAT NICK & HOLLY FOUND IN GRANDPA'S ATTIC
published by Gold 'n' Honey Books
a division of Multnomah Publishers, Inc.

© 1998 by Multnomah Publishers, Inc.
Illustrations © 1998 by José Miralles
International Standard Book Number: 1-57673-372-6

Design by Stephen Gardner

Printed in the United States of America

For information:
MULTNOMAH PUBLISHERS, INC.
POST OFFICE BOX 1720
SISTERS, OREGON 97759

Library of Congress Cataloging-in-Publication Data
Carlson, Melody.
What Nick and Holly found in grandpa's attic / by Melody Carlson.
    p. cm.
Summary: While searching for Christmas ornaments in the attic,
Grandpa, Nick, and Holly find many old objects which remind them of Jesus.
ISBN 1-57673-372-6 (alk. paper)
1. Jesus Christ—Nativity—Juvenile fiction. [1. Jesus Christ—
Nativity—Fiction. 2. Christmas—Fiction.] I. Title.
PZ7.C216637Wh 1998
[E]—dc21   98–14993
                                                    CIP
                                                    AC

99 00 01 02 03 04 — 10 9 8 7 6 5 4 3

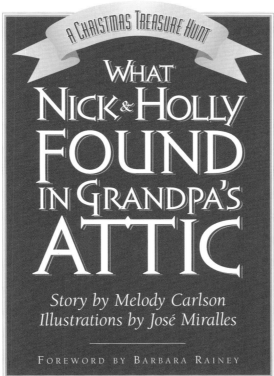

A CHRISTMAS TREASURE HUNT

WHAT NICK & HOLLY FOUND IN GRANDPA'S ATTIC

Story by Melody Carlson
Illustrations by José Miralles

FOREWORD BY BARBARA RAINEY

SISTERS, OREGON

FOREWORD

Too often crowded malls and hectic schedules mark the Christmas season—a time that should be characterized by sweet fellowship with our Savior. That's why I want to challenge families to make room this year for Jesus. By using FamilyLife's Adorenaments (a collection of twelve colorful ornaments that reveal names of Christ) along with the book *What Nick and Holly Found in Grandpa's Attic,* your loved ones can come to know and worship Him more deeply.

As you read of Grandpa dusting off his treasures of long ago, the incomprehensible love of Jesus will be evident. Common objects such as a crib, a dollhouse, and a candle holder will help boys and girls easily visualize names of our Savior such as *Immanuel,* the *Door,* and the *Light of the World*. I believe the Lord will speak to your family in a special way as you turn to specific Scripture passages relating to the names of Christ.

Make room for Jesus this Christmas and begin a family tradition of sharing Adorenaments as you read *What Nick and Holly Found in Grandpa's Attic*. May God use these ministry tools to bring countless children into His eternal kingdom!

Barbara Rainey

Barbara Rainey is a busy wife and mother of six children. She and her husband, Dennis, who is the executive director of FamilyLife, are nationally known speakers and authors. FamilyLife, a division of Campus Crusade for Christ, has been working to bring God's blueprints to families since 1976.

To learn how to order Adorenaments (and other FamilyLife resources), please call 1-800-FL-TODAY.

HOW TO USE THIS BOOK WITH
ADORENAMENTS™

While *What Nick and Holly Found in Grandpa's Attic* can be enjoyed as a stand-alone story, it is designed to be used with FamilyLife's Adorenaments. The goal of the book and Adorenaments is to help children understand that Jesus is more than just a baby in a manger. Through focusing on the names of Jesus, we can help children understand who He is.

Special Christmas traditions serve to bring families together during the hectic holidays. But meaningful family times don't just happen—they take time and planning. By using this book with FamilyLife's Adorenaments, you can create a delightful new Christ-centered tradition for your family this Christmas and for many Christmases to come. You might also consider using this story and the Adorenaments in a Sunday school setting or during a special Christmas celebration with your neighbors.

Open your box of twelve Adorenaments before you read *What Nick and Holly Found in Grandpa's Attic*. Each time the story introduces a new name for Jesus, take out the corresponding ornament and let someone hold it.

When you've finished reading the story, let everyone take turns showing their ornament(s) and reading aloud from the Bible the verses that are printed on the ornaments. Have each person explain in their own words why each ornament is special.

Then take turns placing the ornaments on your Christmas tree. As each person places an ornament on the tree, have them say a simple prayer of thanks, such as: Thank You, Jesus, for being *God with us, the Door, the Vine,* etc.

CHRISTMASTIME

*G*randpa!" cried Holly. "It's *so* beautiful!"

"But what if it doesn't fit in the house?" Nick asked.

Grandpa grinned. "It'll fit, Nick. We'll make it fit!" He leaned the bushy evergreen against the porch rail, then took off his hat and wiped his brow. "This is a fine looking tree. One of the best I've seen in years."

"I just love Christmastime, Grandpa," said Holly with a big sigh.

"And so do I, Holly. But sometimes we get so caught up in the trappings and trimmings that we almost forget what Christmas is all about."

"You mean Jesus' birthday?" asked Nick.

"That's right!" Grandpa put his hat back on. "That's the real reason we celebrate. And now I just hope we can find that box of Christmas tree ornaments. Our attic is so full—it's in need of a good cleaning. But there are so many memories up there that it's hard to get rid of anything."

THE MANGER — GOD WITH US

*T*his is exciting!" Nick said as they climbed the narrow staircase. "We've never been in your attic before, Grandpa."

"Well, then it's high time you were," said Grandpa as he opened the door and turned on the lights. "Now I just hope we can find those ornaments."

"Wow!" exclaimed Holly as she stared at the clutter of trunks, antique furniture, and old toys. "This looks like a fun place to explore!"

"It's like a museum," said Grandpa with a chuckle. "Lots of family history up here."

"Oh, Grandpa, isn't this just the sweetest thing?" Holly asked as she spied an old-fashioned crib.

Grandpa smiled. "My pa built that before I was even born. It's solid cherry wood—the first bed I ever slept in."

"Really?" asked Nick in amazement. "You really slept in this?"

Grandpa nodded. "And so did your mommy." He ran his fingers over the mellow wood. "You know, baby Jesus didn't have a bed nearly so fine when He was born. And He was the Son of God."

"That's right," said Holly wisely. "Baby Jesus slept in a manger. Daddy says that's where you put hay for cows and donkeys to eat."

Grandpa nodded. "Sending Jesus to be born as a baby was God's way of coming down to where we live. That's why Jesus is called 'Immanuel'—that means *God With Us*."

THE DOOR

Grandpa!" cried Holly. "Look at this!" She squatted down to examine an old dollhouse.

"It looks a lot like your house, Grandpa," Nick added, "only way smaller."

Grandpa knelt down beside the dollhouse. "I made this for your mommy when she was a girl." He gently moved the little front door back and forth. "I remember how hard it was to make these tiny hinges for the door."

"And they still work!" said Nick.

Holly bent her head low to peer inside. "I wish I were little enough to walk through this door."

"That reminds me," said Grandpa. "Jesus called Himself *The Door.*"

"Why?" asked Holly.

"Because we must go through Him, like a doorway, to get to heaven."

"Oh," said Nick. "Just like I'd have to go through this door to see the inside of this house. But I can't because I'm too big."

"That's right," said Grandpa. "Unless you could do this." And he lifted the whole roof off the house so the twins could look inside.

"It's beautiful in here," said Holly.

"Heaven will be even more beautiful," said Grandpa wistfully. "I'm glad Jesus made a way for us to get there."

THE VINE

Holly carefully examined the inside of the dollhouse while Grandpa continued to search for the missing box of Christmas ornaments.

"Why, I haven't seen this in years," said Grandpa as he blew a cloud of dust into the air.

"What's that?" Nick came over and studied the painting in Grandpa's hands.

"Your great-grandmother painted this a long time ago," said Grandpa.

"Is it worth a lot of money?" asked Nick with wide eyes.

Grandpa chuckled. "Only to me. You see, my mother painted this when I was young. We had a big grape arbor in our backyard, but it's long gone."

"What happened to it?" asked Holly sadly.

"Well, one year it didn't get pruned. Then there was a hard freeze that broke the branches off. It just never came back after that."

"That's too bad," said Holly. "I like grapes."

"And grape jelly," added Nick.

Grandpa nodded. "Did you know that Jesus said He was *The Vine* and that we're like branches? Jesus wants us to remember all the things He said and keep growing in Him. Then we'll have lots of good fruit."

"Does that mean we're supposed to hold on tight to Jesus?" asked Holly.

"That's exactly what it means," said Grandpa with a big smile.

THE GIVER OF LIVING WATER

"What's this, Grandpa?" asked Nick, pointing to a large pottery jar. "It's a water crock," said Grandpa. "When I was a boy, we didn't have fancy refrigerators like nowadays. We used this clay pot to draw cool water from deep in the well. On a hot August afternoon, sometimes I'd pour a whole jarful of water over my head!"

"Wow! It must've been fun to live back in the good old days," said Nick.

Grandpa grinned. "I can still remember that cool water on a hot day. Well, I'll be. That makes me think of something else we call Jesus."

"What's that, Grandpa?" asked Nick as he held the big crock.

"Jesus is the *Giver of Living Water*. He says if we drink from Him we'll never thirst again."

"But I always get thirsty," said Holly. "Especially in the summer."

Grandpa smiled. "Jesus was talking about our hearts. He fills our hearts with His presence so we don't go thirsting for something else."

"Oh, I think I understand," Holly said, her eyes brightening. "You know what, Grandpa?" she cried. "This is a Christmas treasure hunt!"

Grandpa's eyes twinkled. "And how is that?"

"Well, we were looking for Christmas ornaments, but instead we keep finding these neat old things that remind us of Jesus!"

"I wonder how many more things we can find," said Nick.

"Let's see," said Holly as she began to look around the attic.

THE LIGHT OF THE WORLD

Here's a treasure!" cried Holly as she triumphantly held up an old candle holder with a glass shade.

"I remember that," said Grandpa. "My pa used to carry that out with him when he milked the cows on winter mornings. He'd get up so early it would still be dark outside. Now, that's something I don't miss."

"What's that, Grandpa?" Nick asked.

"Milking those cows!"

Holly laughed. "Yes, but back to the Christmas treasure hunt. This candle holder has something to do with Jesus."

"And what makes you think so?" asked Grandpa.

"Because Jesus is *The Light of the World.* We sing that song in Sunday school all the time."

"Good one, Holly," said Grandpa. "Let's put all our treasures together."

THE BRIGHT MORNING STAR

Here's another treasure!" declared Grandpa. "And, I think I'm getting closer to finding the box of Christmas ornaments."

"What is it, Grandpa?" Nick and Holly asked at the same time.

"See?" said Grandpa as he held out a wooden star. "I made this when your mommy and Uncle Jimmy were kids. We used to put it on our house at Christmastime. I didn't even know we had it anymore."

"Do the lights still work?" asked Nick as he touched the dusty light-bulbs still in place on the wooden star.

"I don't know," said Grandpa, "but we could put some new bulbs in."

"I know what it has to do with Jesus," exclaimed Holly. "It's like the Star of Bethlehem! The one the wise men followed to find baby Jesus!"

"Yes, that's right. But did you know that there's a place in the Bible where Jesus is called *The Bright Morning Star?*"

"What does that mean?" asked Nick.

"Well," Grandpa replied, "a star can be a symbol of hope and direction. You know, stars are like a map that God placed in the sky. Sailors used to navigate by the stars."

"Can we hang this star on the house, Grandpa?" Nick asked eagerly. "It might give people hope and direction about Jesus."

"That's a fine idea, Mr. Nick. Now, what else can we find?"

THE LION OF JUDAH

"Grrrrr!" roared Nick with his hands lifted like claws. Over his face was a lion's mask. "Did I scare you, Grandpa?" he asked as he took off the mask.

"Oh my, yes," said Grandpa; then he laughed. "That mask used to belong to Uncle Jimmy when he was a boy. He used to think he was pretty scary too."

"I can't imagine Uncle Jimmy as a boy," said Holly. "He's so big!"

Grandpa scratched his head in wonder. "Well, I'll be, Nick, my boy. You've gone and found another one!"

"Another Christmas treasure?" asked Holly with excitement.

"That's right. Have you ever heard Jesus called *The Lion of Judah?*"

"No. Is that supposed to be scary?" asked Holly.

"No, but a lion was the symbol of a king, and Jesus belonged to a royal family—the tribe of Judah."

Nick looked puzzled. "What does all that mean, Grandpa?"

Grandpa laughed. "It does sound confusing, doesn't it? Well, the Bible spoke of Jesus long before He was born on earth. You see, God's messengers told how Jesus would be born from the tribe of Judah, and how He would become King, and lots of other things. And that's called prophecy."

THE LAMB OF GOD

O h, Grandpa," sighed Holly. "I think I've found my very favorite treasure." She cuddled a stuffed lamb in her arms and smiled. "He is so soft and sweet."

"That was your mommy's," said Grandpa. "She loved it too."

"Do you think I can keep it?" Holly looked up with big eyes.

"Sure, Holly, I think your mommy would like for you to have it."

"I know what that has to do with Jesus," Nick offered.

Grandpa nodded and sat down in an old rocker. "I'll bet you do."

"I have a picture of Jesus in my bedroom," said Nick. "He's a shepherd with a little lamb just like this in His arms."

"That's right," said Grandpa. "But did you know that Jesus is also called *The Lamb of God?*"

Holly shook her head and looked back down at the fuzzy lamb in her arms.

"He is called the Lamb of God because He's God's Son and He's perfect. But God loves us so much that He gave up His own Son and sent Jesus to earth for us."

"Sort of like the way Mommy loves me so much that she would like me to have her little lamb?" asked Holly.

"Sort of like that," said Grandpa with a smile.

THE GOOD SHEPHERD

"And speaking of lambs," said Grandpa as he reached for a cane that was leaning against the wall, "this old cane reminds me of a shepherd's staff. If a little lamb got caught in thorny bushes, the shepherd used a staff to pull him out."

"And Jesus is our shepherd," proclaimed Nick.

"That's right. Jesus calls Himself *The Good Shepherd*."

"Does that mean there are bad shepherds?" asked Nick.

Holly pulled her lamb a little closer.

"Yes, Jesus warns about shepherds who only pretend to care for the sheep but don't really take good care of them at all. But Jesus loves His sheep so much that He was willing to lay down His life for them."

"And that's why Jesus is my shepherd," said Holly.

"And mine too," added Nick.

"And someday we'll all live together in heaven with Him," Grandpa said.

"We'll get to see Grandma again, right, Grandpa?" Nick asked.

Grandpa's eyes got a little misty. "Yes, child, we'll see Grandma again. And lots of other people who loved Jesus and have already gone to live with Him."

THE KING OF KINGS

*H*ey, Grandpa!" exclaimed Holly, "look at that funny crown." Holly giggled as she placed the chunky crown on Grandpa's head. "Whose crown is this?"

"I think your mommy wore this in a play when she was in high school."

"Are those real jewels?" Holly asked as she touched a shiny bauble.

"No, they're just glass. But guess what."

"Did she find another Christmas treasure?" asked Nick with excitement.

"Yes," Grandpa answered. "This crown reminds me that Jesus is the King."

"Wow. Jesus is so many things, Grandpa," said Nick. "How can we ever remember all of them?"

Grandpa chuckled. "Well, I don't know if we can remember all of them. But I think it's important to remember that Jesus is bigger, higher, and stronger than anyone. And when we think of Him as *The King of kings,* that means He is above everyone and everything else."

"I'll bet His crown has real jewels," said Holly.

"Beyond anything you could imagine," Grandpa agreed.

THE BREAD OF LIFE

Goodness, I haven't seen this for years," said Grandpa. "This is the bread basket my mother used to put on our dinner table every night." He smacked his lips. "I'll never forget the smell of fresh bread baking on a cold winter's day."

"Mmm," said Nick. "You're making me hungry."

"By jingle, we've gone and done it again!" exclaimed Grandpa.

"Another Christmas treasure?" asked Holly.

Grandpa nodded. "Have you ever heard that Jesus is *The Bread of Life?*"

"I think so," Holly answered. "But I'm not sure what it means."

"Me neither," added Nick.

"Well, you know that we can't live without food," Grandpa began.

"Sure, everyone knows that," Nick replied.

"Bread used to be very important. Do you remember how God fed manna to the Israelites in the wilderness?"

"Was manna the same as bread?" asked Holly.

"Yes—a kind of bread. And Jesus miraculously fed bread to thousands of people who came to hear Him teach. Later He called Himself the Bread of Life. He said that if we believe in Him we will never go hungry."

"Is that sort of like Living Water and not being thirsty?" Nick asked.

"Exactly," said Grandpa. "Jesus was talking about a hunger and thirst in our hearts that only He can satisfy."

SAVIOR (THE CROSS)

Here's an easy one," said Nick as he slipped over his head a leather strip with a rough wooden cross tied to it. "Did you make this, Grandpa?"

"No," said Grandpa as he examined the cross. "Uncle Jimmy made it at summer camp when he was a boy. I wonder if he would remember it now."

"Why don't we wrap it up and put it under the tree for him?" Nick suggested.

"That'd be a good gift for Uncle Jimmy," said Grandpa. "The cross is a symbol of the greatest gift that God could ever give."

"You mean because God gave us Jesus?" Holly asked.

"Yes," said Grandpa. "The cross is where Jesus laid down His life so that we could be forgiven. The cross is the place where Jesus became our *Savior*."

"Like when we ask Him to come into our hearts?" Nick asked.

"That's right," said Grandpa. "When we ask Jesus to forgive our sins, we invite Him into our hearts."

Holly touched the wooden cross Nick was wearing. "Did Uncle Jimmy invite Jesus into his heart?"

"He knew about Jesus when he was a boy," said Grandpa with a trace of sadness. "But I'm not sure if he invited Jesus into his heart."

"Do you think this cross might help him think about Jesus again?" Nick asked with a bright smile.

"Maybe so," said Grandpa hopefully. "Maybe so…

THE CHRISTMAS TREASURE HUNT TRADITION

"Hey, what are you three doing up here?" called Jeremy, Holly and Nick's older brother.

"Come on up, Jeremy," said Grandpa. "How was Christmas shopping?"

"Boring," said Jeremy with a big sigh. "Mom said that you were up here looking for the Christmas tree ornaments. But it's taking you forever."

"We were looking for ornaments," said Holly. "But we ended up finding something much better!"

Jeremy stared at the strange collection of objects in the middle of the attic. "What's all this junk for?" he asked as he picked up the crown and placed it on his head.

"This is not junk," declared Nick. "Everything here is very, very special. These are all the things we found on our Christmas treasure hunt."

"What's a Christmas treasure hunt?" asked Jeremy.

"Sit down and we'll tell you all about it, Jeremy," said Nick.

Jeremy sat cross-legged on the floor.

"See this crib?" began Holly. "This is where Grandpa slept when he was a baby."

Nick continued, "But do you know where baby Jesus slept…"

SIMPLE STEPS FOR LEADING CHILDREN TO CHRIST

1. *Be a friend.* Children need to feel comfortable talking about spiritual issues. It's important for children to understand that you're talking to them about Jesus because you love and care about them.

2. *Keep it simple.* The biggest mistake adults make is overcomplicating the gospel. Remember to think like a child. Avoid complicated religious terms. Speak their language.

3. *Let them share.* Give children a chance to tell what they believe, how they feel, what concerns them, and what they wonder about. The more you understand their beliefs and feelings, the better you can share with them.

4. *Talk about Jesus.* Ask them who they think Jesus is and which ornament means the most to them. Explain that Jesus came from heaven and was born as baby, but that He was different than any other person because he was both God and man. Because He lived a perfect life, his death paid for our sins.

5. *Use visual aids.* This book along with Adorenaments will help bring the gospel to life. Children learn better when they see and experience something tangible.

6. *Invite a decision, but be sensitive to God's timing.* If children understand that their sin makes God sad, and if they feel sorry for their sins and want to change, they may be ready to make a commitment. Explain that Jesus can take their sins away and fill their hearts with His love.

7. *Pray with them.* Lead them in a simple prayer by inviting them to repeat each phrase after you:

Jesus, I believe that you are the Son of God and that you died on the cross for my sins. Please forgive me for the wrong things I've done and make me new and clean inside. Thank You, Jesus, for forgiving me. Please fill my heart with Your love and teach me to love and obey You always.

8. *Encourage them.* Explain that all of heaven is rejoicing about their new relationship with Jesus. Show them how excited you are. Tell them that God will send His Holy Spirit to help them. Let them know that they can pray for and receive God's help at any time.

9. *Disciple them.* Teach them that it's important to read their Bible and pray each day. Make sure they have an easy-to-read Bible available. Encourage them to attend church activities where they can learn about God's Word and grow in their faith.

10. *Tell them to tell others.* Encourage them to share their commitment to Jesus by telling their friends and family. This helps to solidify their decision and involves them in sharing the gospel.